SLUG
NEEDS A HUG!

JEANNE WILLIS   TONY ROSS

Andersen Press

Once upon a time-y,
There was a little slimy,
Spotty, shiny, whiny slug.

He was wet and weedy,
Very, very needy,
And always greedy for a hug.

His mummy didn't hug him,
It began to bug him
And he wondered, "Why, oh why?"

"Is she never snuggly
Because I am so ugly?"
said Sluggy with a soggy little sigh.

He spoke to other creatures
With very different features
And asked them what they thought he ought to do

To make himself more huggable,
Less slithery and sluggable
For sadly, Sluggy
didn't have a clue.

"Perhaps if you were furrier
And fluffier and purrier,"
said Kitten, "then your mum
would hug you tight."

So Slug put a woolly hat on
With a picture of a cat on
And a furry jacket, just in case she might.

"You look funny, chummy! If you want a hug from Mummy," said Bird, "you need some feathers and a beak."

Piglet roared with laughter,
"If it's hugs the slug is after
He needs trotters and a tail and a squeak."

With trotters, tail and coat
And beak and feathers, Slug met Goat
Who told him that he looked a little weird . . .

"If you want a hug, my friend
You need horns stuck on the end
And get yourself a handsome goatee beard."

Slug did as Goat suggested
And he sensibly invested
In some horns and a moustache
made out of string . . .

Moth looked aghast and muttered.
And he whispered as he fluttered,
"Slug, you need some wings, you silly little thing!"

Slug made himself a pair.
He couldn't fly into the air,
His wings were scarlet petals from a rose.

Although he smelled delightful
Fox declared that he looked frightful
And he'd never get a hug without a nose.

"Should I lose the beak?" thought Slug,
"If I really want a hug?
Would Mummy love me more with just a snout?"

There was very little space
To wear them both upon his face
But Sluggy did,
    in case of any doubt.

Slug gazed into the brook
At his astonishing new look
And barely recognized
his own reflection . . .

"If she doesn't hug you now,
Then she never will," said Cow
As she gave the slug a head-to-tail inspection.

Hoping Cow was right,
Slug chugged slowly home that night
To show his mum his fabulous disguise . . .

But after all he'd done
She didn't recognize her son.
"Mother, it is me!" said Slug. "Surprise!"

"But I love you as you are!
You're the sweetest slug by far,"
Said Ma, "You have been very greatly missed!
You're beautiful and charming,
If I could, I'd hug you, darling!"

But alas, she had no arms and so . . .

. . . They **kissed!**